A Beginning-to-Read Book

W9-BNJ-494

Dear Dragon Goes to the Library

by Margaret Hillert
Illustrated by David Schimmell

NORWOOD HOUSE PRESS

DEAR CAREGIVER,

The *Beginning-to-Read* series is comprised of carefully written books that extend the collection of classic readers you may remember from your own childhood. Each book features text comprised of common sight words to provide your child ample practice reading the words that appear most frequently in written text. The many additional details in the pictures enhance the story and offer the opportunity for you to help your child expand oral language and develop comprehension.

Begin by reading the story to your child, followed by letting him or her read familiar words and soon your child will be able to read the story independently. At each step of the way, be sure to praise your reader's efforts to build his or her confidence as an independent reader. Discuss the pictures and encourage your child to make connections between the story and his or her own life. At the end of the story, you will find reading activities and a word list that will help your child practice and strengthen beginning reading skills.

Above all, the most important part of the reading experience is to have fun and enjoy it!

Shannon Cannon

Shannon Cannon, Ph.D.
Literacy Consultant

Norwood House Press • P.O. Box 316598 • Chicago, Illinois 60631
For more information about Norwood House Press please visit our website at *www.norwoodhousepress.com* or call 866-565-2900.

Designer: The Design Lab

LIBRARY OF CONGRESS CATALOGING-IN-PUBLICATION DATA
   Hillert, Margaret.
    Dear dragon goes to the library / Margaret Hillert ; illustrated by David Schimmell.
      p. cm. — (A beginning-to-read book)
    Summary: "A boy and his pet dragon go to story time and take out books from the library"—Provided by publisher.
    ISBN-13: 978-1-59953-160-1 (library edition : alk. paper)
    ISBN-10: 1-59953-160-7 (library edition : alk. paper) [1. Dragons—Fiction. 2. Libraries—Fiction. 3. Books and reading—Fiction.] I. Schimmell, David, ill. II. Title.
   PZ7.H558Deg 2008
   [E]—dc22
                      2007037024

Hardcover ISBN: 978-1-59953-160-1   Paperback ISBN: 978-1-60357-082-4

316R—062018
Manufactured in the United States of America in North Mankato, Minnesota.

Come here. Come here.
I want you to help me.
I want you to go
somewhere with me.

I want this
and this
and this
and this.

The red one
and the blue one
and the yellow one.

Help me with this.
We can go now.
We have to walk and walk.

Look there.
See that.
That is where we
want to go.

It is good to go here.
You will see.
It is a good spot.

We have to go up here.

       up.

    up—

Up—

You can do it.

What is this?
This looks like fun.
I want to see this.

Look in here.
See the boys and girls.
They like it there.

We can come in here, too,
but you have to be good.

Where can we go now?
What can we do?

What is in here?
This looks like fun.
I want to do this.

Oh, my.
Look at this.
It looks like you.

And here is something to do, too.

I can do this—
One—two—three.
It is fun to do this.

But now we have to get something
and we have to go.

I want the one that looks like you.
And I want this red one, and
the blue one, and the yellow one.

And this one looks good.
Good, good, GOOD!

Here we go.
Mother will be happy to see us.

Mother, Mother.
Look here.
We have something good.

Here you are with me.
And here I am with you.
Oh, what a good book, dear dragon.

The following activities support the findings of the National Reading Panel that determined the most effective components for reading instruction are: Phonemic Awareness, Phonics, Vocabulary, Fluency, and Text Comprehension.

Phonemic Awareness: Plurals

1. Explain to your child that when a word stands for more than one of something, it is called a plural and that the /s/ sound is added to the word to make it plural. Say the following singular words aloud and ask your child to respond with the plural form:

boy=boys	dragon=dragons	book=books
wagon=wagons	stair=stairs	puzzle=puzzles
kid=kids	bear=bears	chair=chairs

2. Read the plural forms of each word and ask your child to respond with the singular form.

Phonics: Plural Spelling for Words Ending in consonant+y

1. Turn to page 9 and point to the name on the building and read the word library.

2. Ask your child to name the final letter in the word library (y).

3. Ask your child to say the plural word for more than one library (libraries).

4. Fold a sheet of paper in half lengthwise. Draw a line down the center of the paper. Write the word library at the top of the left column and the word libraries at the top of the right column.

5. Ask your child to notice which letters are the same and which letters are different in the two words.

6. Explain to your child that when a singular word ends in a consonant plus **-y**, we need to change the **y** to an **i** and add the letters **es** to make it plural.

7. Write the following words in the left column:

story	baby	puppy	mommy	pony
family	daisy	lady	party	daddy

8. Read each word aloud and ask your child to repeat it.

9. Ask your child to write the plural form of each noun in the right-hand column. Remind your child that she or he needs to change the **y** to an **i** and add **es**.

Vocabulary: Physical Science/Force Words

1. Turn to page 7. Ask your child what the boy is doing (pushing the wagon). Ask your child what the dragon is doing (pulling the wagon).

2. Write the word **push** at the top of a blank sheet of paper and the word **pull** at the top of another blank sheet of paper.

3. Ask your child to draw things that can be pushed on the paper labeled **push** and things that can be pulled on the paper labeled **pull**.

4. Ask your child to name the drawings and label each one.

5. Ask your child to make a complete sentence using the illustrations and labels. (For example: I can pull a wagon.)

6. Examples of pushes and pulls:

Push: swing, chair toward the table, door closed, lawnmower, shopping cart, baby stroller, doorbell, pedals on a bicycle

Pull: rope, chair away from the table, door opened, socks on feet, sled, trailer, a weed from the ground, picking fruit from a tree

Fluency: Shared Reading

1. Reread the story to your child at least two more times while your child tracks the print by running a finger under the words as they are read. Ask your child to read the words he or she knows with you.

2. Reread the story taking turns, alternating readers between sentences or pages.

Text Comprehension: Discussion Time

1. Ask your child to retell the sequence of events in the story.

2. To check comprehension, ask your child the following questions:
   - Where did the boy and the dragon go?
   - What happened when they were there?
   - What kinds of books would you like to check out from the library?

31

WORD LIST

***Dear Dragon Goes to the Library* uses the 61 words listed below.**
This list can be used to practice reading the words that appear in the text. You may wish to write the words on index cards and use them to help your child build automatic word recognition. Regular practice with these words will enhance your child's fluency in reading connected text.

a	dear	I	red	up
am	do	in		
and	dragon	is	see	walk
are		it	something	want
at	fun		somewhere	we
		like	spot	what
be	get	look(s)		where
blue	girls		that	will
book	go	me	the	with
boys	good	Mother	there	
but		my	they	yellow
	happy		this	you
can	have	now	three	
come	help		to	us
	here	oh	too	
		one	two	

ABOUT THE AUTHOR Margaret Hillert has helped millions of children all over the world learn to read independently. She was a first grade teacher for 34 years and during that time started writing books that her students could both gain confidence in reading and enjoy. She wrote well over 100 books for children just learning to read. As a child, she enjoyed writing poetry and continued her poetic writings as an adult for both children and adults.

Photograph by Glenna Washburn

ABOUT THE ADVISOR Dr. Shannon Cannon is an elementary school teacher in Sacramento, California. She has served as a teacher educator in the School of Education at UC Davis, where she also earned her Ph.D. in Language, Literacy, and Culture. As a member of the clinical faculty, she supervised pre-service teachers and taught elementary methods courses in reading, effective teaching, and teacher action research.